MEOW SAID THE COW

By Sarah Mazor
illustrated by Abira Das

THaNK YOU!

ISBN-13:978-1726238250
ISBN-10:1726238253

Silly AUNTIE LILY
Loves cows BIG and SMALL
She tells us cow stories
That make no sense AT ALL

Loony goofy stories
Always told in RHYME
'Cause silly AUNTIE LILY
Is silly all the TIME

I heard a cow say MEOW
I want some food – I want it now

Twittle twattle giggly goo
That is not what cows do

Cats say meow and kittens purr
When you stroke their silky fur

I saw a cow laying eggs
Standing on her strong hind legs

Twittle twattle giggly goo
That is not what cows do

Hens lay eggs some white some brown
Hens have feathers and a crown

I saw a cow shake her mane
Roaring loudly on the plain

Twittle twattle giggly goo
That is not what cows do

Lions roar and have great manes
They live in jungles and on plains

I saw a cow swing on trees
Knocking leaves down with her knees

Twittle twattle giggly goo
That is not what cows do

Monkeys swing on trees and hoot
Bananas are their favorite fruit

I saw a cow swim about
Under water with a trout

Twittle twattle giggly goo
That is not what cows do

Dolphins swim in oceans deep
And surface with a mighty leap

I heard a cow bark at night
It woke me up I jumped with fright

Twittle twattle giggly goo
That is not what cows do

Big dogs small dogs yip and bark
They also play fetch in the park

I saw a cow striped black and white
Eating beans with appetite

Twittle twattle giggly goo
That is not what cows do

Zebras' stripes are white and black
On fruit and beans they like to snack

I saw a cow keeping pace
With three cars speeding in a race

Twittle twattle giggly goo
That is not what cows do

Cheetahs run so quickly by
It sometimes looks like they can fly

I saw a cow build a nest
A cozy place for her to rest

Twittle twattle giggly goo
That is not what cows do

Birds build nests to lay their eggs
Using mud and twigs and pegs

I saw a cow leaping high
Catching with its tongue a fly

Twittle twattle giggly goo
That is not what cows do

Frogs leap high and eat all bugs
They catch dinner with their tongues

I saw a cow stand on one leg
Drinking water from a keg

Twittle twattle giggly goo
That is not what cows do

Storks use one leg when they stand
They make their homes on wet marsh land

I saw a cow sleep nights and days
Until she felt the sun's warm rays

Twittle twattle giggly goo
That is not what cows do

Bears sleep winter months and rise
When spring welcomes sunny skies

I saw a cow hop then stop
To chew some carrots chomp chomp chomp

Twittle twattle giggly goo
That is not what cows do

A bunny rabbit bops and hops
And likes to snack on veggie crops

I saw a cow walk down the road
On her back a heavy load

Twittle twattle giggly goo
That is not what cows do

Donkeys carry on their backs
Loads and loads of heavy sacks

I saw a cow try and squeeze
In a hole while eating cheese

Twittle twattle giggly goo
That is not what cows do

A mouse hides in holes to eat
A yummy yellow cheesy treat

I saw a cow in the creek
Doing nothing for a week

Twittle twattle giggly goo
That is not what cows do

Lazy hippos spend much time
Resting up in swampy slime

I saw a cow roll in sludge
Looking like a chocolate fudge

Twittle twattle giggly goo
That is not what cows do

Pigs are known to roll in muck
Pigs love mud and slime and guck

I saw a cow gather nuts
She tripped over - what a klutz

Twittle twattle giggly goo
That is not what cows do

Squirrels collect nuts all around
Then they hide them in the ground

I heard a cow sing a song
Asking all to sing along

Twittle twattle giggly goo
That is not what cows do

Parrots talk and sing sometimes
They can mimic silly rhymes

Bedtime stories with Auntie Lily:
The READY TO READ Series

More coming soon . . .

**More Books by Author
Sarah Mazor
visit
www.MazorBooks.com**

**More Books by Publisher
Adler's Children's Books
visit
www.SigalAdlerBooks.com**

Made in the USA
Middletown, DE
06 December 2018